Lavender

Lavender

Karen Hesse

Illustrated by Andrew Glass

SCHOLASTIC INC.

New York Toronto London Auckland Sydney
Mexico City New Delhi Hong Kong

I would like to acknowledge my sister, Randy Letzler,
who proved everything could be all right—twice.
—K.H.

ISBN 0-439-17931-9

Text copyright © 1993 by Karen Hesse.
Illustrations copyright © 1993 by Andrew Glass.
All rights reserved.
Published by Scholastic Inc., 555 Broadway, New York, NY 10012,
by arrangement with Henry Holt and Company, Inc.
SCHOLASTIC and associated logos are trademarks
and/or registered trademarks of Scholastic Inc.

12 11 10 9 8 7 6 5 4 3 2   0 1 2 3 4 5/0

Printed in the U.S.A.   40

First Scholastic printing, March 2000

For my aunt, Bernice Millman,
who has always found room for me
——K.H.

For my aunt Dorothy
——A.G.

Contents

1

Sleepover

"Hold on, young lady. Where are you going?" Mom asks.

I put my overnight bag down in the front hall and stand at the edge of the living room.

"It's Saturday," I say. "Sleepover at Aunt Alix's."

"Are you sure Aunt Alix wants you, Codie?" Mom says. "With the baby due so soon?"

"Aunt Alix wants me," I say. "Go ask her."

Mom calls Aunt Alix on the phone. While they talk, I slip into the kitchen and pocket three peanut-butter cookies.

A few minutes later, Mom hangs up. "Aunt Alix says of course you should come. She says to run straight over."

Mom bends down. Her breath smells of peppermint tea. I kiss her on the cheek and pick up my overnight bag. The door bangs shut behind me as Mom calls, "Don't slam the storm door, Codie."

"Sorry, Mom," I call back and head up the block to Aunt Alix's house.

2

Pins and Needles

I practice whistling as I walk up Aunt Alix's path. The dogs leap to the storm door, barking.

From the sewing room, Aunt Alix calls, "Quiet, dogs! Quiet!"

I reach inside my coat pocket and close my hand over the peanut-butter cookies.

"Here, Gina. Here, Lance. Here, Tracy," I say, opening the door and stepping in.

Aunt Alix lumbers up the steps from the sewing room, a dressmaker pin clasped in her lips.

I worry about that pin.

"What if you swallow it?" I ask. "What if the pin sticks the baby?"

Aunt Alix's eyes tell me the pin will not stick the baby. But she takes it from her mouth and pokes

it into her wrist cushion all the same.

Up in Aunt Alix's muddled living room, the dogs gobble their peanut-butter cookies. Settling on the lumpy sofa, they lick the crumbs from one another's whiskers.

"How's my cousin doing?" I ask. I put my ear to Aunt Alix's belly.

"Swimmingly," says Aunt Alix.

Aunt Alix pretends it's easy having a baby, but I know it isn't always. Aunt Alix has tried having a baby lots of times. This is the closest she's come to a baby fully done.

Aunt Alix's baby will be my first cousin.

Mom and Aunt Alix have dozens of cousins. It's about time I had one, too.

3

Make Room for Codie

I follow Aunt Alix down to the sewing room.

Folds of flannel hang over the ironing board. Fabrics spill from the shelves.

Aunt Alix is pinning a skirt on Eleanor, the headless mannequin. I hold up the waist of the skirt and hand Aunt Alix pins.

"Is this for Mrs. Zobris?" I ask. Aunt Alix makes most of Mrs. Zobris's clothes.

"Yes," says Aunt Alix, adjusting the waistband.

It takes longer than usual with the pinning. When we finish, Aunt Alix eases down into her chair.

"Thanks for your help, Codie," she says, reaching out for me.

Aunt Alix holds me close against her big, hard

belly where the baby is growing.

I stretch my arms around her middle and try to hug back. Aunt Alix's belly gets in the way.

"Hey," I say to my cousin inside Aunt Alix, "make room for me."

Aunt Alix says, "There will always be room for you, Codie."

And she means it.

4

Baby Things

Aunt Alix sits at her sewing machine. I sit on the stool beside her.

Picking up a long strip of silky fabric, I rub it between my fingers.

"What's this for?" I ask.

"It's for the baby," Aunt Alix says.

She shows me the tiny clothes she has sewn. They are mostly in different shades of purple.

"Are you all ready for the baby, then?" I ask.

"Not quite," says Aunt Alix. "I won't be fully ready until the blanket is done."

I have a secret. I am making my cousin a blanket all by myself. It's a surprise.

"What kind of blanket are you making?" I ask. I hold my breath.

"Oh, I'll just use that remnant of flannel," Aunt Alix says. "And trim it with the lavender ribbon." Lavender is Aunt Alix's favorite color.

I'm making Aunt Alix's baby a blanket from material out of the scrap box. It's a crazy mixed-up quilt to go with Aunt Alix's crazy mixed-up house.

"I have plenty time to make a blanket, though, Codie," Aunt Alix says. "The baby's not due for two more weeks. First things first."

Aunt Alix slides the seam of Mrs. Zobris's skirt under the fingers of her sewing machine. She touches her foot to the pedal and the motor hums.

5

Making Music

Aunt Alix leans forward. The sewing machine sings its rubbing song. Its silver tooth races up and down. Fabric creeps forward out of Aunt Alix's lap, folding itself against the back wall. I free the material whenever it gets caught on something.

The radio plays overhead. Aunt Alix and I sing along.

When we don't know the words, we make some up.

> *"Cream-colored ponies,*
> *and cold apple noodles,*
> *cowbells and dumbbells,*
> *and spaniels and poodles."*

Suddenly Aunt Alix straightens in her chair. "What's wrong?" I ask.

Aunt Alix looks down at her belly. "Your cousin just kicked me."

I see the baby glide under Aunt Alix's shirt.

"That's not kicking, Aunt Alix," I say. "That's dancing."

While Aunt Alix works at her machine, I practice my hand sewing on some scraps.

I'm sewing my cousin's blanket by hand, too. I've packed it in my overnight bag to work on when Aunt Alix and Uncle Chuck think I'm asleep. At home, I work on the quilt in my room, with the door closed. Not even Mom knows about it.

And I'm nearly done, I have mostly the trim around the edges left. I can easily finish in two weeks.

•

6

French Toast

Just before dark, a motorcycle roars up. Uncle Chuck's big voice booms down the steps. "Anybody home? Alix!"

"Be right up," Aunt Alix calls. She finishes the seam she's working on, slides the skirt out from under the sewing machine's fingers, and snips the threads.

Climbing the steps slowly, Aunt Alix rubs the hollow place at the bottom of her back. I take the steps two at a time behind her.

"Hey, Uncle Chuck," I call.

Uncle Chuck fills the hallway with the smell of leather.

"Hey, Codie."

Gina and Lance and Tracy dance around Uncle Chuck's legs. He tosses me his helmet, hooks the

14

dogs on three leashes, and takes them for a run.

I dodge around the sculptures in the living room and help Aunt Alix start dinner.

We fix French toast.

Uncle Chuck sets the table with cinnamon and syrup and pale yellow butter.

"Where's the powdered sugar?" Aunt Alix calls.

Uncle Chuck leaps across the kitchen, pinching his big fingers inside the sugar box and sprinkling the sweet white dust over Aunt Alix and me.

We have a sugar fight, blowing white clouds that float through the air. Sugar tickles my cheeks, and my eyelashes, and inside my nose. I lick my lips and the sticky corners of my mouth.

That night, tucked into my cot, I hear Aunt Alix and Uncle Chuck's voices drift up the stairs. Opening my overnight bag, I pull out the top and the bottom of my cousin's quilt. I trace the velvety patches with my fingers and sigh. Aunt Alix's house smells of powdered sugar, hot griddle, and coffee.

7

It's Time

Sometime during the night I hear Aunt Alix calling from downstairs, and then a lot of bumping around. Suddenly Uncle Chuck's face appears at my doorway. "It's time, Codie!"

I get up on my elbow. "Time?" I ask, but Uncle Chuck has already disappeared.

The dogs race around the house, barking wildly. I listen for Aunt Alix to call out, "Quiet, dogs! Quiet!" but she doesn't. After a few seconds, the dogs quiet down all by themselves.

Then my mom walks in. She's wearing her coat over her bathrobe. Her hair looks night-wild.

"Mom?" I ask. "How come you're here?"

"Uncle Chuck called, Codie," Mom says. "It's time—for the baby."

"No, it's not. Aunt Alix says two more weeks."

Uncle Chuck tears past the door with a big suit-case and flies down the steps.

"The baby says now," insists Mom.

I worry about Aunt Alix. I worry about my cousin, too. I know it's not good if the baby comes too soon. Is it still too soon?

I race down the stairs after Uncle Chuck, dodging the sculptures, and pushing past the dogs to get to the front door.

Outside, in the dark, Uncle Chuck holds on to Aunt Alix's elbow. She walks stiffly down the path, like she's ice walking, but there's no ice.

A big white moon hangs over their heads. Uncle Chuck tucks Aunt Alix into the car and they speed away.

8

Trimming the Night

Climbing the stairs, I look for Mom. She is stripping the sheets off Aunt Alix's bed.

"We'll let this air overnight and make up the bed fresh tomorrow," Mom says.

"Is Aunt Alix going to be all right?" I ask.

"Of course," Mom says.

"And my cousin?"

"Your cousin, too."

Mom never lies. She never lies.

"Come on, Codie. It's late," Mom says, yawning. "Let's curl up together on the cot."

I hear cars rumble past outside. Creaking-house sounds pop out of the darkness.

Mom's arm grows heavy on top of me. She is asleep. How can she sleep while Aunt Alix is having the baby?

I wiggle out from under Mom's arm and lean toward the window. My skin touches the cold glass and I shiver.

Suddenly I remember the blanket!

The baby doesn't have a blanket.

Aunt Alix can't have her baby yet.

Hold on, Aunt Alix.

I pull the almost finished quilt out of my overnight bag and tiptoe down the steps, and down the steps again, to the sewing room.

Eleanor's headless body spooks me. I don't like being alone with her.

But I have to finish the blanket. Aunt Alix didn't have time to make one. And she said she wouldn't be ready until the blanket was done. If the blanket's not done, maybe the baby's not done either.

But if I can finish *my* blanket, if *my* blanket is fully done, then maybe the baby will be fully done, too. And everything will be all right.

Aunt Alix would use her sewing machine to make the blanket. That would go much faster. But

the silver tooth worries me. What if it sews my hands together?

I spread the top and bottom of my cousin's quilt on the floor, good sides facing out.

"Eleanor—" I look up at Aunt Alix's mannequin. Everything feels so strange without Aunt Alix here. Eleanor stands over me wearing nothing but Mrs. Zobris's skirt. "You see this blanket, Eleanor?" I say. "I'm finishing it tonight."

I start by lining up the top and bottom of my cousin's quilt, trimming the edges so the two pieces fit. Then I fix the pieces together with pins at each corner and another in the center.

Pulling the blanket into my lap, I even up the purple and gold and green jumble of fabrics.

Finally, I pin Aunt Alix's lavender trim along the edges. It is hard pushing the needle through all those layers. It hurts my fingers. And my stitches are big and sloppy and they don't always go where I want them. Sometimes I miss the trim altogether. Other times I catch my pajamas, and have to tear them free.

"Do you think Aunt Alix will notice the messy spots?" I ask Eleanor, studying my uneven stitches. But even a headless mannequin can see I haven't done the trim right.

And it has to be right, for Aunt Alix, for the baby.

Using the seam ripper, I pull out the bad stitches and start again. Aunt Alix's thimble wiggles on my finger like a loose tooth. I hold it in place with my thumb and keep working.

My eyes get blurry and my shoulders burn, but I have to finish.

I keep rethreading the needle every time I go around a corner of the blanket, and sometimes even before.

But finally I am coming up the last side, closer and closer to the end. And then I push the needle through the thickest layers of all, and it's done. I tie a knot, and snip the threads, and the blanket is done.

Fully done.

And it's perfectly beautiful.

* * *

I am careful to take all the pins out. I wouldn't want any to stick my cousin.

I fold the blanket, carry it upstairs, and tuck it away in my overnight bag. Mom snores softly.

It's late and I want to lie down, but I have no place to go. Mom fills the whole cot. We've stripped Aunt Alix's bed. There is no room for me.

Aunt Alix said there would always be room for me. But Aunt Alix isn't here. If Aunt Alix were here she'd find room for me. I know she would.

I go down to the living room and settle myself on the lumpy sofa. Lance sticks his wet nose in my face and nuzzles my cheek.

"Don't worry, Lancie," I say. "The blanket is done. Aunt Alix and the baby will be all right."

9

It's a Color

When the phone rings, Mom is standing with her back to me, coddling eggs at Aunt Alix's stove.

"Would you answer that please, Codie?" Mom asks, her hands all eggy.

The voice on the phone is Aunt Alix. She sounds like she's calling from under the sea.

"It's a girl," Aunt Alix crows. "A beautiful, healthy girl."

"Hooray! It's a girl," I tell Mom.

"Lovely," Mom says.

"Is she fully done?" I ask.

"Perfectly," Aunt Alix answers.

I think proudly of the blanket upstairs, tucked inside my overnight bag.

"What did you name her, Aunt Alix?"

"Lavender," Aunt Alix says.

"Lavender?"

"Yes," says Aunt Alix. "Don't you like it, Codie?"

"It's a color," I say.

"Exactly," says Aunt Alix.

"When is she coming home?" I ask.

"Tomorrow, Codie," Aunt Alix says. "All three of us. I can't wait for you to see her."

"I can't wait, either," I say. "Good-bye, Aunt Alix."

"Let me have the phone," Mom says, putting two quivery eggs in front of me.

Lavender, I think, trying the name out as I bite off a corner of toast.

At last, I have a fully done cousin. A perfectly, fully done cousin—named Lavender.

10

Preparations

I walk the dogs, one at a time, while Mom washes up from breakfast. We clean Aunt Alix's house, front to back, top to bottom.

I carry upstairs all the tiny clothes Aunt Alix has made for Lavender. Mom tucks them into the dresser drawers.

We go to the market and buy baby powder and ointment and diapers and a blue rubber thing.

"What's that for?" I ask.

"That sucks the gunk out of the baby's nose," Mom says.

"Why doesn't Lavender blow her nose?" I ask.

"Babies can't," Mom says.

"Oh."

* * *

We drive over to the hospital after shopping. Mom asks at the desk in the lobby for Aunt Alix's room.

As the elevator climbs, I stoop to pull up my socks. Mom uses a wet fingertip and rubs at a smudge on my face.

I expect Aunt Alix to meet us as soon as the elevator doors open. Instead, two nurses are coming down the hallway. One of them goes behind a wall of glass, but the other stops in front of us.

"May I help you?" she asks.

"I'm here to see my sister," Mom says. "Alixandra Moore."

"Ah, yes," the nurse says. "And who is this young lady?"

She looks down at me.

"I'm Codie," I say.

"My daughter," says Mom.

"I'm going to meet my cousin," I say, starting down the hall.

"Not so fast," says the nurse. "We have a room for you to wait in, Codie."

"I don't need to wait," I tell the nurse. "I'm going to see my cousin now."

The nurse says, "I'm sorry, but you can't. Children aren't allowed. Hospital rules."

I look at Mom.

"Maybe Aunt Alix and Lavender can come out to see you," she says.

The nurse leads me to a sitting room with green plastic sofas and some books with their covers ripped off.

I've always been able to see Aunt Alix any time I wanted. Why can't I see her now?

I stand at the edge of the room, waiting, expecting Aunt Alix to come around the corner any moment.

But she doesn't come. A few minutes later, Mom appears.

"All three of them asleep," she says. "Aunt Alix in her bed, Lavender in her basket, and Uncle Chuck in a big stuffed chair. Come on, then, Codie. We'll see them at home tomorrow. That's not too long to wait."

"Are you sure they're all right?" I ask.

"They're fine," Mom says. "Perfectly fine."

Back at Aunt Alix's house, we put fresh sheets on the bed and fresh flowers in a vase. I smooth the cot so there isn't one wrinkle.

When I'm certain Mom is all done in my cousin's room, I pull out the quilt from my overnight bag. I look at it one last time, touching the velvety greens, the silky purples. Fully done, I think.

I bury my face in the blanket. It smells of Aunt Alix's sewing room.

I try spreading the quilt neatly inside Lavender's crib, but my arms aren't long enough. It only looks messy.

I have another idea.

Folded into the top dresser drawer, Lavender's quilt covers the tiny clothes Aunt Alix has made. My heart whips madly, thinking about Aunt Alix when she finds what I've done for her.

Sunlight pours through the curtains of my cousin's room. I think the room wants Lavender to come home as much as I do.

11

The Baby

The next morning, back in my own bed, I wake up early. This is the day I meet my cousin. I check for Aunt Alix's car. It's not back yet.

"Why don't you go over and take care of the dogs?" Mom asks.

"Okay," I say, slipping into my clothes.

I feed the dogs, and take them for their walks.

Upstairs, Lavender's room looks perfect. I peek in the top drawer and touch the blanket once more. Then I go to the front window and wait.

Finally, Uncle Chuck, Aunt Alix, and the baby come home. Aunt Alix carries the baby in a little fuzzy sleeping bag. Between Mom, the dogs, and Uncle Chuck, I can't even get close.

"Hi, Codie," Aunt Alix calls from across the room and blows me a kiss.

I go feathery inside. My heart taps hard against my ribs and my face burns. Everything feels changed. Even with Aunt Alix here.

I try to see my cousin, but I can't. I try to see Aunt Alix, but I can't do that either. Aunt Alix promised there would always be room for me. She promised. But it doesn't feel like it now. It doesn't feel like there's nearly enough room.

I am feeding Lance and Tracy and Gina cookies when Aunt Alix comes up behind me.

"Did you think I forgot you?" Aunt Alix asks.

It's easier to hug her now. My arms wrap nearly all the way around her middle.

"Would you like to see your cousin?"

"Oh, yes!" I say.

I follow Aunt Alix up the stairs.

We peer through the crib slats, together.
I catch my breath.

Is this my cousin?

It's so red, and wrinkly, and bald. And so little. Just a lump, curled up tight. Tiny, shriveled feet poke out from under its nightgown. It makes little snorting noises.

"Oh," I say.

"Isn't she lovely?" Aunt Alix asks.

Aunt Alix can't mean this baby. Not this baby.

That scrubby lump in the crib could never be my cousin.

12

Lavender

We stare at the baby a long time. It keeps grunting and then it starts to squeal. Aunt Alix lifts the baby out of the crib. Its legs stay curled up inside its nightshirt. The baby isn't very big, but I feel like it takes up the entire room.

Gently, Aunt Alix places the baby on the pad covering the top of the dresser. She changes its diaper. The baby has a sore-looking stump where its belly button ought to be.

"Do you know where your mom put the ointment?" Aunt Alix asks.

She opens the top drawer of the dresser, looking for belly-button medicine.

She finds the quilt I made instead.

Slowly, Aunt Alix lifts the blanket from the

drawer. She holds it up, turning it over, then over again.

"Codie?" Aunt Alix asks. "Where did this come from?"

"I made it," I say. "For you and for Lavender."

"Oh, Codie," Aunt Alix says. Her voice sounds sweet and light, like powdered sugar.

My heart taps hard against my chest. I can't look at Aunt Alix. I watch the baby instead, making sure it doesn't roll off the dresser.

It punches itself in the face with its fist, but it doesn't cry. It starts sucking on the back of its hand. What a funny thing to do.

"Shall we see how she looks in your quilt?" Aunt Alix asks.

Aunt Alix wraps the baby in my blanket. Then, carefully, so carefully, she lowers Lavender into my arms. The baby looks up at me. It yawns wide and crosses its eyes. The lavender edge of the blanket falls down around its puffy face. I hold the baby, consider her. It still feels like she takes up the entire room, but it isn't a bad sort of taking.

"She'll love this quilt forever, Codie," Aunt Alix says, kneeling beside me.

"She won't be little like this forever, though, will she?" I ask.

Aunt Alix smiles. "She'll get bigger every day."

Aunt Alix strokes the lavender trim with her fingers. The baby's face turns when the blanket touches her cheek.

"Thank you, Codie," Aunt Alix says.

"Do you really like the quilt?" I ask.

"I think it's lovely," Aunt Alix says, placing her arm around my middle.

I look at Aunt Alix. I look at my new cousin.

"I think Lavender is lovely, too," I say.

And I mean it.